Roaming Riley

A Baltimore Adventure

ALLISON WIEST

ISBN 978-1-62806-337-0 (print | paperback)

Library of Congress Control Number 2021922081

Published by Salt Water Media
29 Broad Street, Suite 104
Berlin, MD 21811
www.saltwatermedia.com

Cover art and illustrations by Tracey Arvidson
Chapter illustrations by Madelyn Wiest

Visit the author's website: www.allisonwiest.com

Dedication

For my daughters, Anna and Madelyn:

I love you most.

∞

Mom

Chapter 1
Adventure Awaits

"Why can't we go, Daddy?" Rosie asks as she waves a wand in the air for me. I leap up and flip around. There's a bright yellow feather at the end of the wand and I really want to catch it. Rosie's sister, Nicki, laughs at my failed attempt.

"My business trip is on a weekday this time, sweetheart. You girls have to go to school. The school year just started," Dad says as he folds a pair of pants and adds them to his suitcase.

"But you're staying with Aunt Kristin. She's so much more fun than going to school," Nicki whines, trying to convince her dad to take them along.

Dad laughs and pulls Nicki's braids, making her giggle. "I'm sure she is, but school is your job just like my work is mine. You and your sister need to stay here and help your mom while I'm gone. I know she doesn't like it when I have to stay over-night. You can keep her company," Dad says as he puts the last of his clothes in the suitcase.

Rosie flips the feather up and down, around and around. Finally, I jump high enough to snatch it. Proud of my success, I pull the feather

over to Dad's freshly packed suitcase and climb onto the clothes with the wand dragging along behind me.

"Guess what, Riley!" Rosie says excitedly. "You don't have to hide in the suitcase this time!"

"Yeah!" Nicki says. "Dad is taking you along so he doesn't get lonely. We bought a comfy cat seat for the car so you can ride as a passenger this time."

My ears perk up as I listen to the girls and I quickly forget about eating the feather. Could this really be true? I know Dad enjoyed having me with him on his last trip, but is he really taking me on another adventure? Going to Delmarva was the most exciting experience I have ever had. I met so many new friends and explored lots of towns. Could I do that again in a new place? I meow at Dad and look at him questioningly.

"You heard right," Dad says, scratching my head. "You're going to be my traveling partner again. This time we are headed to Baltimore City so not too far from home. You'll get to hang out with some animal friends, too."

"Rick and Duane!" Nicki exclaims.

"You're going to love them," Rosie says as she pets me. "Rick is the cutest little dog and Duane is a cat just like you! You can all play together and then watch the birds out the window.

Sorry, Jack, you aren't going on the trip with Riley. You get to stay and play with us," she explains as my brother cat slowly walks into the room. I can tell right away that he's stalking me and wants to play. I crouch down and wave my tail back and forth.

"Looks like the boys want to play before we leave," Dad says, zipping up his suitcase. "Girls, come help me get the car packed up and then I'll get my traveling buddy."

Jack and I watch Rosie, Nicki, and Dad leave the room and then the fun begins. Jack pounces on me and we roll around the floor batting at one another. After a few tumbles, he pins me to the ground.

"So, did I hear right? You get to go on another adventure?" Jack asks as I desperately try to break free.

"That's right," I reply. "Dad's taking me to Baltimore to stay with Aunt Kristin, Uncle Mike, and their pets," I say as I escape from Jack's grip and jump onto the bed.

Jack notices the feather and decides it's more interesting to play with than attacking me. I watch as he bats it around with his paw and then chews on it.

"Everything you told me about your Delmarva adventure sounded so cool," Jack says. "You should explore Baltimore and see what it's like."

I look down at him thoughtfully. "That's exactly what Bagel told me to do. Before he flew away, he told me to find friends and explore. It was so easy to do in Ocean City since I could just sit on the balcony and then climb down. What will I do in Baltimore? How will I be able to get out?" I ask.

"Oh, you're resourceful. You'll find a way," Jack says, jumping up on the bed with me. "Maybe one day I will get to go on a trip with you too," he adds, sounding a little jealous.

"I never expected that you'd want to," I reply. "I thought you just liked to sleep all day."

"I do love sleeping," Jack says as he curls up against a pillow, purring.

I laugh as he closes his eyes. "Enjoy your nap, Jack," I say, leaping off the bed. It's time to get ready for my adventure!

Chapter 2
Cruising

"How do you like your seat? A little better than being stuck in a suitcase, huh Riley?" Dad asks, glancing over at me as he drives down the highway.

A LITTLE better?! This new seat is incredible! Nicki and Rosie weren't kidding when they said how comfy it is. Dad strapped it onto the passenger seat up front next to him. It has a fluffy cushion that sits up high so I can see over the dashboard and out the window. I am mesmerized. On our trip to Delmarva all I saw was the big, scary bridge before I settled down into the suitcase. Now I get to watch the whole world fly by! I've never seen so many different vehicles before. There are small cars just like ours and big ones too, in every color you can imagine. A bright orange jeep drives past us and it looks just like a giant pumpkin from Halloween. Buildings and trees whiz by on the side of the road. I even watch as a plane takes off into the sky. Suddenly, a loud horn makes me jump and burrow down into my cat seat.

"Don't be scared, Riley," Dad says, petting me reassuringly. "That's just a truck. It's a lot bigger than our car, but we'll be past it in a minute."

I peer out the window skeptically as we drive next to the giant truck. Dad's still petting me so I feel a little better, but it sure is big

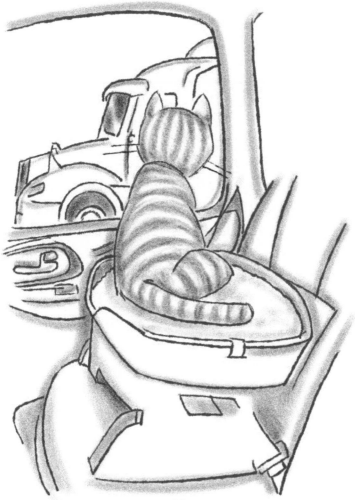

compared to our car. When we reach the front of the truck, the driver does a double take as he sees me, a little orange tabby cat, looking up at him. Laughing, he waves at me and I decide to be brave. I press my front paws up against the window and wag my tail a little, hoping he can see it.

"Are you sure you aren't part dog, Riley?" Dad asks, laughing as I continue to lean against the window. Traveling like this is much more fun than being cooped up in a suitcase. People smile and wave at me as we drive by, making me feel like a celebrity. I meow at dad to let him know I am happy.

"All better now?" Dad asks, understanding my cat language. He scratches behind my ear, just where I like it best. "We'll be at Aunt Kristin's in about half an hour. Let's see if we can listen to the Orioles game as we drive," he says, changing the station on the radio. The sound of the announcer's voice is the last thing I hear before I settle into the cozy seat for a catnap.

"It's the top of the sixth and the Orioles are up 5-3. The count is three and two with two outs. Runners are on first and third, hoping to score and tie up the game. Akin winds up and pitches a curveball. It's a swing and a miss! The O's stay on top, heading into the bottom of the inning."

Chapter 3
A New Tour
Guide

"Here we are, Riley," I hear Dad say as I lazily open one eye. I was having the best dream about eating french fries. I look around and notice the car isn't moving anymore. Instead we are parked in front of what looks like a bunch of houses all connected in a row. Aunt Kristin walks out of one of the front doors with a little brown dog. He hasn't noticed me yet so I am able to get a good look at him first from the safety of my car seat. He is a small dog, just a little bigger than I am. He is very excited to see Dad—I can tell by how his tail is wagging—and his bark makes a 'woo woo woo' sound. Considering all he wants to do is lick Dad all over, I think he might be friendly.

Dad opens the trunk of his car to get his suitcase and Aunt Kristin walks over to the window where I am. "What's the best way to introduce them?" Dad asks, joining her at my window.

"I'll keep Rick out here for a few minutes while you take Riley inside. Let him scope the place out and meet Duane first before I let Rick run wild," she says.

Dad takes his bags inside and then comes back out for me. It's a short walk from the car into the house, so he carries me into the foyer and sits me on the ground.

"Here's where we're staying for the night, Riley. Check it out."

This house is completely different from ours. There is a big set of steps just inside the front door. I slowly make my way up, unsure of what I might find at the top. I can smell dog and cat in here and the cat smell gets stronger as I reach the top of the stairs. I peer around the corner and see a cat who I assume is Duane. He must have heard me coming because he's perched up on top of the sofa where he can look down at me. He's a small cat with completely black fur except for little bits of white on his paws. His yellow eyes are watching me intently as I come further into the room. I think about all of the animal friends I met on my last trip and decide to be brave.

"Hi! I'm Riley. You must be Duane. I'm excited to be here," I say as I cautiously walk over to him. I hope he's nice, but you never know.

Duane looks at me a moment and then jumps down to sniff me. "Hey, Riley. What's your story? People visit here all the time, but they always bring their dogs, never their cats. How'd you get to make the trip?"

"Well, the last time Dad went on a business trip I fell asleep in his suitcase and ended up in Ocean City with him. He liked having me there so much, he decided to bring me along this time."

"That's pretty cool. What did you do while he was working all day?"

"Funny you should ask," I replied. "I planned to sleep on the balcony all day, but then a local seagull named Bagel woke me up. We ended up

spending the day together touring the whole area, up and down the Eastern Shore. It was awesome!"

Duane smiles mischievously. "Oh, we're going to get along really well. One of my favorite things to do is wander around Baltimore. We can head out tomorrow morning when everyone goes to work. That's what I usually do. I overheard Mom talking about going to the Orioles game tomorrow night with your dad, so they won't be home until late. I can show you all the sights around my town. We have some of the most delicious food too," he adds, licking his lips.

"Duane, that would be amazing!" I say excitedly. I can't believe it. This day just keeps getting better and better. I've been here five minutes and already have a new friend and a tour guide. Duane and I start batting at each other playfully when I hear the front door open.

"Here comes Rick," Aunt Kristin yells up the steps.

My defensive instincts kick in as Rick races into the room. I can tell he wants to play with me, but I'm not ready for that without getting to know him first. I jump up on a table so he can't reach me and stare down at him, just like Duane did when I entered the room.

"I'm Rick," he says, wagging his tail frantically. "You must be Riley. My mom has been telling me all about you."

"Don't be afraid, Riley," Duane says reassuringly. "Rick is harmless. He likes to play, eat, and sleep, kind of like us. What do you say we show him what it's like to play with two cats instead of just one?" he says, smiling playfully again.

I wag my tail in response and then we both get into stalking positions. Rick looks at Duane and then back at me, unsure of what's about to happen. Just as he decides he should run away, we pounce simultaneously. Duane and I chase him up the stairs, down the stairs, around the kitchen table, and back into the living room. Duane and Rick jump at each other a few times while I play with Rick's tail. Finally exhausted, Rick curls up in his dog bed for a nap and Duane and I lie on the top of the couch.

"This is the best place to look at the birds," Duane tells me. We watch them for a few minutes and then eventually curl up together sleepily.

"It looks like they've decided to be friends," I hear Dad say to Aunt Kristin as I happily drift off to sleep.

Chapter 4
Charm City, Here
We Come!

"Have fun and don't torment Rick too much," Dad says as he rubs my head. Morning has come and he is getting ready to go to meetings all day. Aunt Kristin is going to drop him off and then head to the vet hospital where she works as a veterinarian.

"We won't be back until late tonight," Aunt Kristin says. "Our neighbor is going to stop by to fill your food bowls, so don't worry. You won't starve. We'll be back as soon as the O's beat the Red Sox. The Ravens are playing the Steelers this afternoon too, but that crowd should be gone before our baseball game," she tells Dad.

"Crazy that they're playing this afternoon, but I guess that's what happens when half the team gets sick from Covid and they keep postponing. You can't just cancel a Ravens/Steelers game," Dad says as he gathers up his things for work. I'm only half-listening. I am so anxious for them to leave. Once they're gone my adventure with Duane can begin.

"No, you absolutely cannot! They're one of the best rivalries to watch," Aunt Kristin replies, grabbing her purse and heading down the stairs with Dad. "Have fun guys!" she calls up to us.

Duane and I walk to the top of the stairs and watch as Dad and Aunt Kristin leave through the front door. His tail is wagging a little and I can tell he's just as excited as I am. I follow him as he races back to the window and we watch the car drive away.

"What are you two crazy cats doing?" Rick asks, watching us curiously.

"Heading out for another adventure, Rick," Duane tells him as he climbs onto the back of the sofa. "Turns out Riley loves to explore just as much as I do. I'm going to show him around the city and maybe even check out the O's game later."

"Make sure you grab some of Boog Powell's pit beef while you're there. Mom dropped some once and I gobbled it up before she could grab it. It was delicious," Rick says, licking his lips.

"What's a Boog?" I ask puzzled.

Duane laughs. "Just wait, new friend. By the time we get home tonight, you'll know exactly what a Boog is. Now let's break out of here!"

I jump up on the sofa next to Duane and

watch as he gets to work. Aunt Kristin left the window open so we could get fresh air inside today. Duane takes his paw and puts it right in the corner of the screen. Using his claws, he carefully peels the screen back just enough that a cat can fit through it.

"Hmm," Duane says, looking thoughtfully at me. "How are we going to get you out? I usually jump from here over to that tree branch. I can jump really far. It's kind of a superpower of mine," he says proudly.

A superpower? Have I really found another cat with special abilities just like me? "Duane, that's amazing! I can't believe you have a superpower because I have one too. Two, actually. I can climb up and down walls and I can run super fast. I never told you how I really got out of the hotel room back in Ocean City. Bagel found me up on the balcony and then I climbed all the way down the side of the hotel! If you jump over to the tree, then I can just climb out and down behind you."

"No way! That's super cool, Riley. Let's not waste any more time. Rick, you know what to do, right?"

"I sure do, Duane. Once you're both out, I'll carefully push the screen back down so it looks like you never left," Rick explains to me.

"You really do this a lot, don't you, Duane?" I laugh as we get ready to escape. "I wish you could come too, Rick. I hate having to leave you behind."

"It's ok. Just be ready to tell me all of your stories when you get back later. Have fun!"

"Thanks, Rick! Alright, Riley, once I'm out you can join me," Duane says. Without hesitation he leaps from the window and lands perfectly on the tree branch. I watch as he continues to jump from branch to branch until he's settled on the ground. Alright, I think to myself. Time to show off my special powers. Carefully, I dig my claws into the wall outside the window and begin my descent. I can hear Duane cheering me on from down below. When I get close to the ground, I jump off and land next to him.

"Whoa, Riley! That was awesome!" Duane says, giving me a high five with his paw. "With your ability to climb and mine to jump, the possibilities are endless for what we can do today. Let's go! I want you to meet a friend of mine first. It's not too far, so we can just walk."

Duane and I walk down the street and then onto some back roads. While we walk, I talk more about my trip to Delmarva and the exciting things I saw there. He laughs when I tell him how I got from one place to another—driving a

scooter, a jet ski, riding on a dolphin, and everything else. After a short walk, he stops.

"Here we are. Charm City Vet Hospital. My mom is the owner! We have to be really careful since she could be back here at any time. If we're lucky she's still dropping your dad off at his meetings. I just wanted you to meet my friend, Arnold. He is a three-legged cat who spent a lot of his younger years exploring Baltimore. Maybe he can tell us his can't-miss places to go today," Duane says.

We walk together to the front of the vet hospital and resting in a window is an orange tabby cat. As we walk toward the window, he gets up slowly, yawns, and stretches.

"Hey, Duane. Good to see you. Who's your pal?" Arnold asks, checking me out.

"Hi there, Arnold. This is my cousin, Riley. He's visiting today and I'm going to show him all around Baltimore."

"Hi, Arnold," I say. "How did you get that name?"

"Well, since I only have 3 legs, one of them is similar to a peg-leg, just like a pirate has," he explains. When I still look confused he continues, "Do you know a pirate's favorite letter?" I shake my head no and he answers, "Arrrgh!"

I laugh and reply, "So, 'arrrgh' turned into Arnold, huh?"

"You got it! Arrrghn't you glad you asked? Now, where are you guys going to go today?" Arnold asks when we all stop giggling.

"Well, I know I want to start at Fort McHenry and then walk around the Inner Harbor. Later I

might take him to the Orioles game. Where else would you suggest?" Duane asks.

"I heard some clients inside talking about the Fells Point Festival. That must be going on this week. There will be a lot of people there so nobody will notice two cats walking around. Oooh, and you have to go to Little Italy for cannolis!" Arnold adds, licking his lips.

"Sounds like we're going to do some serious eating today," I say to my new friends. "I'm starting to love this city already!"

"Great ideas, Arnold. Sorry to cut this short, but we have to be on our way or we're going to miss the boat," Duane says. I don't know what boat he's talking about, but I've learned to just go with the flow.

"Say hi to the guys at the dock for me," Arnold says. "Well, or at least meow a lot since they can't understand you!"

"Great meeting you, Arnold. I hope I see you again sometime. Meow to Aunt Kristin for me," I say, laughing as Duane and I begin walking away.

"Off to our first adventure!" Duane shouts as we run together toward the water. He's pretty speedy too. I can already tell it's going to be a fantastic day!

Chapter 5
Hop To It!

"Here we are," Duane says. We are standing on a dock and looking out across a river. "This is the Patapsco River. It starts at the Inner Harbor in downtown Baltimore and flows all the way to the Chesapeake Bay. That's the bay you crossed when you went over the giant bridge to Ocean City," he explains.

Thinking of that bridge makes me shudder. "How are we going to cross the river, Duane? You said by boat, but are we going to drive it or is someone going to drive us?"

Duane laughs, "Someone's going to drive us this time, Riley, but maybe we can find something for us to drive later. There's a nice lady here at the dock who lets me ride on her sailboat sometimes. Here she comes now." Duane points to a woman who is already smiling at him as she walks toward the water.

"Looking for a boat ride, kitty? You picked a gorgeous day for one. Looks like you brought a friend with you too, huh? The more the merrier!" she says as she scratches Duane, pets me on the head, and then hops into a boat with Baltimore Hon written on the side of it.

Duane and I follow her onto the boat and I take a minute to look around. This boat is a lot bigger than the one that took me to Assateague Island on my last trip. It has a huge white sail pointing up to the sky. I walk around the deck and find a spot to curl up and take a nap. My eyes have just fluttered closed when I feel a paw whack me on the back of the head.

"What do you think you're doing down there?" Duane asks.

"Um, sleeping?" I reply, rubbing my head. "Why did you smack me?"

"You don't sleep on a sailboat, Riley. There's too much to see! Come follow me and I'll show you how it's done."

Reluctantly, I leave my cozy sleeping spot and follow Duane to the middle of the boat. He looks back at me with a grin and then begins jumping from beam to beam until he's at the top of the mast that's holding the sail. The old Riley would have said no way, but I'm brave Riley now. Without giving it another thought, I climb up and follow Duane all the way to the top of the mast. We both cling to it tightly as the woman starts to direct the boat away from shore.

"What do you think?" Duane calls out to me after we have been sailing for a few minutes.

"What an unbelievable view!" I shout back. I look around and take in all the sights. It's a beautiful day and there are many other boats on the water. Way down below, there are a few fishing boats and a speedy motorboat. As we cruise along the river, we pass another sailboat and I see a seagull perched on the top of the sail. I can't help but wonder if he knows my

good friend, Bagel, from Ocean City. I smile to myself thinking of him. Before long, up ahead I see what looks like a huge green park with a giant star on it. I have never seen anything like it. As I gaze at it wondering what it could be, Duane seems to read my mind.

"That's our destination, Riley," he says, pointing at the big star-shaped area. "It's called Fort McHenry and it's been there since the 1700s. That's the first place we'll explore today."

As our sailboat docks at the shoreline, Duane and I climb back down the mast, meow goodbye to the nice lady who brought us here, and head across the greenest grass I've ever seen toward Fort McHenry. All of a sudden, I stop in my tracks as a bunny darts quickly past me and then hides by one of the walls, staring at me with big, round eyes.

"Hi!" I say in my friendliest voice. I can tell that the rabbit is really scared and probably doesn't talk to many cats. Now here he is faced with two scary-looking felines. "My name is Riley and this is my cousin, Duane. We are going to explore Fort McHenry today."

Cautiously, the rabbit hops a little closer. "I've never met a cat who didn't chase me," he says, looking from me to Duane and then back to me. He clearly doesn't trust us.

Duane sits down in the grass and looks at me, encouraging me to do the same. I assume he's trying to make the rabbit feel more comfortable. I sit down also and purr a little for good measure.

"We're different from other cats," Duane tells our new furry friend. "We like to explore and make new friends. My cousin, Riley, is visiting Baltimore today with his dad and I'm acting as his tour guide. I want to show him around Fort McHenry, but I don't know everything about it. Could you help us?"

As Duane is talking I can tell that the rabbit is relaxing a bit because his ears aren't sticking straight up anymore. Finally, he smiles and says, "I've lived here all my life and spend most of my days hopping around the fort. I would

be honored to be your guide today. My name is Poppy."

"It's great to meet you, Poppy," I say, moving close enough that I can rub my tail against her to say hello. "Where is a good place to start exploring?"

"There's a spot in the fence over here that I can squeeze through easily, but I'm not sure about you guys. Can you jump?"

"I can jump and Riley can climb," Duane tells her. "Lead the way!"

We follow Poppy toward the water and over to a fence that encircles the giant star. As she goes through, Duane leaps over it and I climb up and then down. There's a path that leads into the star so we make our way along it together.

"This is called Fort McHenry now, but it wasn't always known as that," Poppy says, giving us some background. "Way back during the Revolutionary War, a small fort was built here called Fort Whetstone. Almost 25 years later, Fort McHenry was constructed to protect the harbor and it's been in this spot ever since. During the War of 1812, a famous poet named Francis Scott Key wrote the country's national anthem, 'The Star-Spangled Banner,' after watching the British bomb the fort. He was amazed to see the American flag still flying the next morning, so he wrote a poem about it that eventually became our anthem."

"Oh! That must be why it's shaped like a huge star, right Poppy?" I ask excitedly.

"That's a good guess, Riley, but that's not why. The original builders designed it as a star so that soldiers could easily keep watch in all directions. Throughout the years, the fort has been used for all kinds of things. It's been a hospital, a place to train the military, and even a prison!"

"Wow, a prison? Are there any prisoners here still?" Duane asks nervously.

"No, not anymore. It isn't used for any of those things now. It's a national park, so lots of visitors come to see it, explore, and learn about its history. That's how I know so much. I've been on a lot of tours in my time," Poppy says. "You know—"

Poppy's next words are cut off by the loudest sound I've ever heard. Duane and I both jump, our hair stands on end, and our claws come out. We look around frantically for either a place to hide or something to attack. Then I notice Poppy laughing at us.

"Poppy, what was that? Are we ok?" I ask.

Still laughing, Poppy replies, "We're fine, Riley. Relax, Duane, and put your claws away, both of you. One of the tour guides must be demonstrating how to fire a musket. That's all."

"A musket? What's that? Is that like a muskrat? I've heard those are tasty," Duane says.

"Sorry to burst your bubble, Duane, but you can't eat it. A musket is a long type of weapon that was used during the wars. People who work here show tourists how they work and what they sound like. We're safe," she reassures us. "If we stay close by the walls, then nobody should notice us. Let's go find the crowd and see what they're up to."

Together, we move toward the sound of the musket. Before long, we're in the middle of the fort and a group of people is standing in a circle around a flagpole. We inch as close as possible to see what's going on.

"Every morning, we raise the flag to start our day," the tour guide announces to the crowd. "We remember everyone who fought here to protect our country and the anthem that symbolizes our freedom."

"Let's get closer," I whisper to my friends. I want to see what this flag raising is all about. Since everyone is facing the flag, nobody seems to care about a few cats and a rabbit as we make our way to the front.

The man continues, "All I need is a volunteer to help me. Is this anyone's first time visiting Fort McHenry?"

Me! Me! I think in my head. Except I must not have thought it. I meowed it! All eyes turn to me, including Duane's and Poppy's. Most look shocked while others seem amused.

"What do we have here?" the man asks. "It looks like a few patriotic animals have decided to join us today, folks. Hey there, Poppy. It's good to see you again. Looks like you've found some friends. I can't believe I'm saying this, but how would you kitties like to help me raise the flag this morning?" As he says this, he waves a rope around in the air, tempting us.

Like the playful cats we are, Duane and I spring into action, trying to grab the rope. The crowd erupts into roars of laughter as we jump, meow, and bat at the rope. Finally, I catch it in my teeth and smile at the audience who applauds my success.

"Well done, little man. Now, let's fly this flag."

As the man begins to pull the rope, I reluctantly let go. Duane and I watch in awe as the red, white, and blue masterpiece rises slowly into the air. When it reaches the top, the crowd falls silent and everyone puts their hand over their heart as the national anthem begins to play. I listen and make a memory of how beautiful a moment it is. The flag is waving gently with the breeze and is framed by the blue sky with the sun shining brightly on it. As the song comes to an end, the crowd applauds once again while Duane and I meow as loudly as we can. I can tell he was also mesmerized by the ceremony.

"Thanks for helping!" the man says to us before leading the crowd to another part of the fort.

"That was incredible!" Poppy says as we rejoin her on the grass. "I've seen a lot of flag raising ceremonies in my life, but it's always young boys and girls who get to help, not cats!"

"That was a cool experience," Duane says. "I'd say that was the perfect way to start our day, Riley. I think it's time to explore more of the city, though."

"Where are you headed next?" Poppy asks.

"Well, I'd like to take him over to the Inner Harbor, but I'm not sure of the best way to get there."

"Oh, that's easy. Just hop on the Charm City Circulator," Poppy says as if we have any idea what that is. When we look at her with blank faces, she continues. "It's just a shuttle. It's a type of bus and it's free for people, so I would assume it's free for cats too. It will take you right into the downtown area. Let's go!"

We follow Poppy to the bus stop and a shuttle is already there loading with people. "I've ridden something like this before, Duane. Only I climbed on top and rode on the roof," I tell him.

"Sounds good to me. Let's climb up and get seated before it takes off. Poppy, thanks for showing us around Fort McHenry," Duane says, rubbing his head against Poppy's floppy ear to say goodbye.

"Yeah, thanks Poppy! That was really neat and I'll always remember that giant star," I say.

"It was great to meet you guys. I'll think of you every time they raise the flag and play the anthem," Poppy says. "Have fun exploring and be careful!"

Duane and I climb quickly to the top of the shuttle and lie down just in the nick of time. The Circulator takes off, swiftly carrying us to the next leg of our journey!

Chapter 6
View From Above

"This is wild!" Duane shouts as we ride through the city on top of the Circulator. It really is an amazing way to travel. All of those people inside the shuttle are really missing out. As we move through the busy downtown traffic, Duane begins to point out the sights to me.

"That's Federal Hill," he says as we pass a park and a taller mound of grass. "It's a whole neighborhood now, but back during the Civil War it was used as a fort by the Union Army."

"Kind of like how Fort McHenry was used?" I ask.

"Exactly! You're already learning a lot today, Riley. Poppy was a good teacher. I had never actually talked to a rabbit before."

"I hadn't either. I met a lot of cool animals when I visited Delmarva though. I already told you about Bagel. He's a seagull. I also met a pony, dolphin, skate, and crab!" I am happy to tell Duane about the friends I met on my trip. I know they'd be so excited to hear about what I'm doing in Baltimore today.

"Mmmm, crab is so good! Did you know

Baltimore is well-known for its crab cakes? We have the best in the whole world! We can find some later for lunch if you want," Duane says.

"I couldn't possibly eat a crab!" I exclaim, horrified at the thought. "My friend Cuddles was a crab and he stayed with me for most of my adventures. I just couldn't!"

Duane laughs, "No worries, buddy. Maybe we can find some crab-flavored chips instead. I promise they aren't made with crab," he adds when he sees I still look disgusted. Before long the Circulator stops to unload its passengers. We climb down from the roof and Duane leads me along the sidewalk until we get to a big open area with the most delicious smells. People are all around shopping, eating, and enjoying the city on a beautiful day.

"It's our lucky day, Riley," Duane says suddenly. "Someone must have dropped their bag of chips. Come check these out." He sits down and instantly begins snacking.

I inspect one of the chips and then sniff it. Big mistake! I begin sneezing instantly. Duane howls with laughter and I know right away what it must be.

"These have Old Bay on them, don't they?" I ask, licking one carefully.

"They sure do. It's the greatest seasoning

around. How do you know about it?"

"When I was in Ocean City, it was on top of my ice cream. Hey, these chips are delicious," I reply as I join him for a snack.

"Ice cream? I never would have thought to put it on that. I bet it was good though. You can't go wrong with Old Bay." Finishing his chips, Duane stands up and stretches. "You ready, Riley? I want to show you what the city looks like from up above."

"From a plane?" I ask, looking curiously at the sky.

"Haha, no, but that sure would be a fun adventure sometime. I'm talking about from up there. That's the World Trade Center," Duane points to the top of a building. It has five sides like Fort McHenry, but where the fort was low to the ground, this building shoots way up into the sky.

"I'm not sure that's much safer than an airplane," I say hesitantly as we walk toward the tower.

"What happened to the brave cat that rides on top of buses and climbs up and down buildings?" Duane asks jokingly. "Believe me, it's safe and the view will be worth it. I've sneaked in before to look around. What's great right now is that it's closed to the public, so as long as we can find a way in we'll have the whole floor to ourselves."

"Alright, Duane. I will have to trust you," I say, not wanting to look like a coward.

"That's the spirit! Now let's get inside and then I have an idea about how we can get to the top. The offices are still open so people should be inside. We can hide in a corner and wait for someone to come off the elevator. Before the door closes, we'll run inside and be on our way," Duane explains.

"That's a great idea, but how do we get

inside?" I ask as we arrive at the front of the building. There are regular doors on the sides, but in the middle is a giant circular door I've never seen before.

"Wait until you see this, Riley. Watch me and then follow me in!" Duane says and takes off into the round door. He puts his paws against the glass window and the door begins to spin. Suddenly I don't see him anymore. He must be inside somehow, I think to myself. I'll have to do the same thing if I want to join him. I wait for the door to stop spinning and step inside. I tap my paw gently against the window. Nothing happens. I look up, down, and around for an idea of what to do.

"Push harder!" I hear Duane call to me from inside the building. Here goes nothing, I think and then I push with all my might. The door starts spinning slowly. As I push harder, it begins to move more quickly. As I continue to push, I see Duane sitting and waiting for me. I smile at him as I keep pushing and going around in circles. I'm starting to get dizzy but I'm not sure how to get to where Duane is. As if reading my mind, he calls out to me again.

"When it comes around, jump out! You'll be fine. I promise!"

Trusting my cousin, I wait for the door to spin and then I jump right onto Duane. We tumble around on the floor and land against the wall in a heap.

"So much for staying quiet," Duane laughs as we shake ourselves out.

"That was like an amusement park ride!" I tell him. "I once went on these teacups that spin around in circles and make you really dizzy. That's how I just felt."

"When we leave you can ride it again," Duane says. "Get ready. I just heard the elevator bell ding. We'll only have a few seconds to get on once the passengers exit."

Quietly, we crouch down into ready positions. The doors open and two businessmen walk out talking about where they're going to eat lunch. As soon as we know they can't see us, we dart onto the elevator just as the doors are closing. I've never been inside an elevator before. I watch as Duane presses number 27 with his paw and then we start to move. The elevator starts going up, but my stomach goes down, just like when I'm on a roller coaster. It doesn't take long before the bell dings again and we've reached our destination.

"Welcome to the 'Top of the World!'" Duane announces as the doors open. I can't believe my eyes. Windows wrap around the perimeter of the pentagon-shaped room. From this height, I can see the entire city of Baltimore and beyond. Binoculars are set up in different parts of the room and Duane leads me to one of them. I watch as he climbs up and peers through it.

"What do you see?" I ask him.

"From here I can see where we just were at Fort McHenry. This one is pointing to the southeast," he says before giving me a turn. I look through and everything is magnified. I can see the flag flying that we raised earlier this morning. I look around but can't see Poppy!

"Take a look over here," Duane calls from across the room. As I join him, he points out into the distance. "That's the Basilica of the

Assumption also known as the Baltimore Basilica. It's so pretty inside. It was built back in the 1800s and is the first Roman Catholic Cathedral in the whole country. It's not too far from Lexington Market. They have the best crab, I mean food, there," he corrects himself, remembering how I feel about eating crab.

"What's that big park out there?" I ask, pointing toward the northwest.

"That's the Maryland Zoo in Baltimore. I've heard Mom talk about it before. All different kinds of animals live there. Even polar bears!"

"Wow! I bet we could make all kinds of animal friends there," I say.

"I bet we could, but that's a little far for our adventures today," Duane says, moving closer

to the window and looking down. "I want to take you by that submarine next and then over to the aquarium. Considering your last trip was to the beach, I think you're going to love seeing the marine animals."

Looking down, I see what looks like an angry shark in the water next to a funny triangle-shaped building with a glass roof. "Duane, I don't like the looks of that shark," I say nervously.

"Don't worry, Riley. That's just a submarine. It's just like a boat, but it goes under the water instead of on top of it. All the sharks in the aquarium are in tanks so they can't hurt us. What do you say we head over there now?"

"Ok, if you say so," I reply, following Duane back to the elevator. Sharks inside a tank might not be so bad. What could go wrong?

Chapter 7
Submarines and
Sharks

It's a lot easier to get out of the World Trade Center than it was to get inside. Duane and I ride down the elevator and only spin around the revolving door two times for fun before we are outside again. Duane leads me along the harbor toward the angry shark. I try to remember that it's not real, but those white painted teeth sure do look sharp!

"This is the USS Torsk," Duane says once we're next to the submarine.

"Torsk? What a funny name," I reply. "What does it mean?"

"It's Norwegian for cod which is a type of fish. A really tasty fish," he adds, licking his lips.

"Oh! Is it named for a fish because it goes underwater?" I ask.

"That's right! Long ago, submarines had all kinds of water animal names. This one here is from the mid-1900s. It was used all over the world, from Florida to Hawaii, Japan to Connecticut and many places in between."

"Wow! Was it ever in any wars?"

"Actually, yes. It was used during World War II. It even fired a couple torpedoes. If you thought that musket this morning was loud, I can't even imagine how loud a torpedo would be," Duane says.

"The sailors must have been really brave," I say.

"They absolutely were," Duane agrees. "Hey, here's our next stop, the National Aquarium," Duane says as we get to the triangle-shaped building. Up ahead there's a group of children who must be on a field trip. Their teacher is giving them instructions about how to act once they get inside.

"I have an idea," I tell Duane. "What if we join that group of kids up there? We can find people who like cats and act cute so they take us in with them."

"That's an excellent idea, Riley. How about those two girls?" Duane says, pointing. "One of them is wearing cat ears, so she must like cats!"

"Sounds good to me. Let's go!"

We walk over to the girls who are listening to their teacher. I hear Duane meow quietly and I gently rub my tail against one of the girl's legs.

"Oh! Jenny, look! Two adorable kitty cats! Hello, sweet kitty. Aren't you just the most precious little thing?" she says as she reaches down to pet me.

"Aw, Kiara, they are so cute! This little black and white one is so soft," she says as she begins petting Duane.

"I have an orange tabby cat just like you at home," Kiara tells me as I do figure eights around her legs. "I wish we didn't have to go inside and leave you two out here."

Just then the teacher announces that it's time to go explore the aquarium. Duane and I both meow sadly and look up at the girls with wide eyes.

"Jenny, we can't just leave them out here. Let's take them inside!" Kiara says excitedly. Duane and I look at one another in disbelief. Our plan is working!

"Kiara, that's crazy! Don't you think we'll get in trouble?" Jenny replies, looking unsure.

"We can't get in trouble if they just happen to run in while we have the door open," Kiara says mischievously. "Come on, guys. We'll let you in, but then you have to stay out of trouble inside the aquarium. Follow us!"

"Ok, but if Mrs. Getzinger catches us, we're in big trouble," Jenny replies.

The girls run to catch up with their classmates while Duane and I stay right beside them. As they go through the entrance, we hide between their legs and walk straight into the aquarium.

"Wow, Duane. This is incredible," I say as I look all around. In the middle of the lobby is a giant tank with familiar animals swimming inside. "Those look a lot like skates. Did I tell you I surfed the ocean waves on a skate named Barny? Maybe one of these guys knows him."

"Nothing surprises me about you, Riley," Duane says. "It sounds like you had quite an adventure on Delmarva. Let's go ask one of them."

We get as close to the tank as we can and peer in. These animals seem bigger than Barny and smoother. Their tails are long and skinny with what look like stingers on them. One of them notices us and swims over.

"Who are you guys? We see a lot of people in here, but never other animals just walking around. I'm Monty," he says.

"I'm Riley and this is Duane. We came in with those students and are exploring the aquarium," I tell him.

"That's so cool! I wish I could explore. I couldn't tell you the last time I was out of this tank. I spend all of my time swimming around here with the other rays," he says.

"You're a ray?" I ask him. "You look a lot like my friend, Barny. He's a skate who lives in the Atlantic Ocean. I surfed the waves on him once," I say proudly.

"Wow! Surfing the waves sounds gnarly, dude. I've heard of skates but never met one before. They're similar to us, but they don't have these cool stingers on their tails," he says, thrashing his tail around to show us.

"Whoa! Watch where you whip that thing!" Duane says, backing away a little to keep from getting stung.

"Sorry!" Monty says, calming his tail. "Where are you headed next?"

"We'll start at the bottom and work our way up, I think," Duane says.

"Fun! That means you get to start with the

sharks. Don't worry, Riley," he says, seeing my frightened face. "They're in a tank like me, but even more protected. They're harmless."

"I can't wait," I say sarcastically.

Monty laughs, "You'll be fine. Thanks for stopping by my tank. Have fun today!"

"Bye, Monty," we say as he swims away with his friends. The girls and their classmates are making their way toward the sharks so we follow along behind them. I can see another tank ahead of us, but this one is entirely enclosed just like Monty said. There's a sign that says "Shark Alley." I try to put on a brave face as we get closer.

"It's ok to be scared, Riley," Duane says reassuringly. "Even though I know we're safe, I'm still a little nervous too. What do you say we make a game of it? Their names are written here. If we have fun with those, then they won't seem so scary."

"What do you mean? How can we have fun with their names?" I ask as a giant shark swims toward the glass.

"Look at this one coming over here now. It's called a Largetooth Sawfish. Hey, Largetooth!" Duane calls toward the shark. "I need some wood cut for my fireplace. Want to give me a hand with that later? You can saw it for me!" He erupts into giggles as the shark swims away.

"I love it, Duane! Let me try," I look at the next shark about to swim by and read its name. "Hello there, Nurse Shark. Where are all of your patients today? Want to take my temperature?" We laugh again as the shark swims off. Duane is right. This makes being around sharks a lot less scary. In no time at all, we reach the end of the alley.

"We made it! See, I told you it wouldn't be so bad," Duane says, putting his paw around me. "Now, let's go check out the less frightening animals."

Chapter 8
Sink or Swim

We follow the school group through the rest of the exhibits which are much less terrifying than the sharks. I can't believe how many different kinds of fish there are and that we aren't allowed to taste any of them! As we walk past tanks, a lot of animals stop and stare at us. I guess they've never seen animals walking around here before, just like Monty said. The only animals that don't seem to care about us are the snakes who all appear to be sleeping.

"These are some of my favorite animals," Duane says as we get closer to an animal I've never seen before. It's kind of like a fish, but it has a curvy tail.

"It says here that it's a Longsnout Seahorse," I tell Duane. "I've met a horse before and she didn't look like this."

"You're right, Riley. They look a lot different from the horses that run around outside. It says here that their heads are similar to horses' heads, but I can't tell. Let's peer in a little closer."

We move to the edge of the tank and put our front paws up on the railing. Duane is a little taller than I am so he can see over the top. Maybe if I push off a little, I think to myself, then I'll be able to see inside too. I crouch down just a bit and push off with more force than I mean to. Splash! I am stronger than I thought! One minute I'm outside of the tank and the next I'm swimming with the fishies!

"Riley!! Can you swim?!" Duane shouts.

Can I swim? I have no idea but I am going to have to figure it out if I want to get out of this tank. I kick my legs around and feel my body start to move. I'm swimming! I turn my head around and find myself nose to nose with a seahorse.

"New to the tank?" he asks me jokingly as I flail my body around.

58

"You could say that," I reply. "I was just trying to get a closer look and fell in."

"I'd say this is as close as you can get," he laughs. "I'm Andy. Need some help getting out?"

"I'm Riley and yes! Please lead the way!"

Andy swims effortlessly to the side of the tank while my long legs propel me forward, splashing all around. I'm able to climb up and out of the tank and back to dry land.

"Thanks for showing me the way, Andy," I say as the seahorse swims away.

"Riley, that was amazing! I've never even tried to swim. You looked like you really knew what you were doing," Duane says.

"It was sink or swim," I reply, shaking water out of my fur. "I didn't know I could do it either, but I didn't have much of a choice. Thank goodness it was a tank full of seahorses and not sharks!"

As I continue to dry myself out, we hear a voice over the loudspeaker announce, "The dolphin show will begin in approximately 10 minutes. Everyone come find a seat!"

"Dolphin show? I rode on a dolphin when I was in Ocean City," I tell Duane excitedly. "Let's go see what this is all about."

We follow a large group of people who are

headed toward the amphitheater for the show. "Let's see if we can get close. Come this way," Duane says, heading away from the seats and down some steps toward the water. Duane pulls me back against a wall when one of the dolphin trainers rushes past. Fortunately, he doesn't see us. All of a sudden, one of the dolphins swims close to the edge and spots us.

"Whatcha doing over there?" he asks in a squeaky voice. "I've never seen cats in here before. Are you a new part of the show?"

"Hi! I'm Riley and this is Duane. We sneaked into the aquarium and have been exploring ever since. We aren't part of the show, but I have met a dolphin before," I tell him.

"Really? Here in the aquarium?" he asks.

"No. I actually met him in the Atlantic Ocean. His name is Bo and he gave me a ride on his back from Ocean City, Maryland all the way up to Lewes, Delaware."

"No way! What a coincidence! I'm a bottlenose dolphin from the Atlantic also, but I haven't been there for a long time. My name is Nate. It's nice to meet you," he says, waving his tail at us. "What about you? Do you ride dolphins too?" he asks Duane.

"Sadly, I've never been to the ocean. You're the first dolphin I've ever met," Duane replies.

"Well, you boys are in for a treat today. What do you say we show the audience something they've never seen before? That is, if you're okay with getting just a little wet," Nate says with a grin.

Duane laughs, "Riley here already went for a swim today, so I guess I should get wet too."

"What happened to you?" Nate asks.

"I had a very close encounter with a seahorse," I reply, laughing and shaking out my damp fur.

"Sounds like you're a pro then," Nate laughs. "Alright, here's my plan. You two stay out of sight over here while we do the normal part of the show. In a while, our trainer will announce that we can show off any way we please. That's when I'll come and get you. Sound good?"

"Why not?" I answer and Duane agrees.

"If Riley can swim, then I probably can too," he says.

"The only way you'll have to swim is if I throw you off my back, so don't worry. Enjoy the show," Nate says, splashing us with his tail as he dives away. Right then, the trainers start the show by announcing the dolphins. Nate is joined by two others who amaze us by jumping into the air, diving for toys, leaping through hoops, and splashing the audience. Duane and

I laugh along with the crowd as the animals do their tricks. Before long, I hear one of the trainers tell the dolphins it's their turn to show off.

"That's our cue," Duane says as we see Nate swimming over to where we are hiding.

"Ready to be stars?" Nate asks. He swims parallel to the wall, waiting for us to join him.

"Here goes nothing," Duane says. We climb onto Nate's back and hold on tightly to his dorsal fin as he takes off through the water.

He skims along the top so we won't get drenched, bouncing up and down like a jet ski.

"Whee!" I yell. I hear the crowd laughing and shouting. I get a glimpse of the trainer's face and her mouth is open in disbelief. When she told her dolphins to show off, I don't think this is what she had in mind.

"Having fun?" Nate asks as he speeds around in circles.

"This is the most fun I've ever had," Duane tells him and I nod in agreement. We're going so fast it's hard to speak.

"Hold on tightly for the grand finale," he tells us. "Hold your breath, too."

We don't have time to think about what that could mean. Nate swims into the middle of the pool, thrashes his tail, and leaps into the air. He spins around in three circles before diving back down into the water. We're completely submerged for a brief second and then Nate brings us back to the wall. Duane and I climb off and hear thunderous applause from the crowd. I look up and see Jenny and Kiara pointing and waving at us. If they hadn't let us in, then we wouldn't have been part of this incredible show!

"Let's give one more round of applause to our dolphins, especially Nate and his new feline friends," the announcer says as we shake ourselves out.

"I think it's about time we dry out and get some lunch. I've worked up an appetite. Want to go find some sunshine and snacks?" Duane asks.

My stomach growls loudly in reply. "I guess that means yes," I say, laughing. "Thanks for the fun ride, Nate!" I call as he swims back to join the others.

"Anytime, Riley! Bye, Duane!" he says, waving his tail at us. We head toward a sign that says exit, leaving the aquarium behind and moving on to our next adventure.

Chapter 9
A Killer Day

"What did you say this place is called?" I ask Duane. We are walking through downtown Baltimore to find lunch. Duane said it wasn't far, but I'm a little scared of the cars whizzing by.

"Little Italy. The pasta there is so delicious you'll think you are actually in Italy. And wait until we get dessert," Duane says.

We cross the street and find ourselves in what seems like a whole new world. Trees and old brick buildings line the streets. People are sitting outside, eating, shopping, and enjoying the beautiful day. The most amazing smell fills my nose and my tummy growls again.

"Almost there, buddy," Duane says, recognizing my hunger. "If we go around back we might be able to find some leftover pasta." He leads me behind one of the restaurants and the aroma gets stronger.

"This smells a lot like the pizza I ate in Bethany Beach," I tell him.

"Mmm, pizza is tasty, but today you have to try authentic pasta and meatballs," Duane says as he scrounges around in the dumpster. "Aha! I knew we'd find leftovers. Crazy humans are always throwing away food like this."

I join Duane and dig in. He wasn't kidding. The sauce is full of flavor and the meatballs are heavenly. I have fun slurping the spaghetti noodles which makes Duane laugh. We've been so busy today, I didn't realize how hungry I was.

"Where to next, Duane?" I ask, licking sauce off my paws as we finish our meal.

"First, we need to make our way over to Vaccaro's. They have the best desserts in town. If we're lucky maybe we can find a cannoli to eat. After that, more exploring! If we keep going a couple blocks, then we'll get to another town similar to this one. It's called Fells Point and there's a really cool festival happening there today. That's what Arnold was telling us about," he says, finishing the last of his meatballs.

"Sounds good to me. Let's go!"

Duane leads me over to Vaccaro's where we easily find dessert. I can't believe anyone would throw away food so sweet, decadent, and delicious. Bellies full, we make our way over to Fells Point. Along the way, Duane points out St. Leo's Catholic Church, which is right in the center of Little Italy. We get close enough to see that it has been around since the 1800s according to one of its stones. As we continue on our way, the aroma of marinara sauce follows us. After a few blocks, it disappears and instead I'm struck by the noise. Music, talking, laughing, and even dogs barking greets us as we enter the town.

"Welcome to the Fells Point Festival!" Duane announces. "It started as a way to save the town and now it's grown to be a fun time for everyone. It brings a lot of money in too which helps the area. Check out those people walking by," he says, pointing to a group of women. I've never seen anything like them. They all have on pointy glasses, boas draped around their shoulders, and their hair is wrapped up high on their heads like a beehive.

"Is it a costume party?" I ask Duane.

"They're what we call Baltimore Hons. It's a hard thing to explain, but you see them around town for festivals like this one," he explains. "Oh, look! There's a whole group of dogs over there. Want to go see what's happening?"

"Sure," I say, as we make our way over to them. Rick was friendly, but I'm not sure about these dogs. There are all different kinds: big, small, calm, crazy, and everything in between. Duane bravely walks right up to them, acting as if we belong.

"Hey, guys! What's going on? Enjoying the festival?" he asks as if he's one of the gang.

The dogs look at us and do a double take. "Who are you?" asks a big golden retriever.

"I'm Duane and this is my cousin, Riley. We're exploring the whole city today and thought we'd check out the fun festival. I didn't expect to see a bunch of dogs. Are you here just for fun too?"

"Exploring the city on your own? That sounds wonderful," she says. "Our owners brought us down here today to be part of the pet parade. I've participated every year since I've lived with them. People line the streets and throw treats at us. It's super fun. My name is Chessie because I'm a Chesapeake Bay Retriever."

"Nice to meet you, Chessie," I reply. "Can we join the parade? That sounds like fun!"

"I don't see why not," she says. "I have a

great idea. Us bigger dogs usually pull a cart in the front with a Pet Parade sign on it. What if you two ride along on the cart? I'm sure the crowd has never seen anything like that before."

"Count us in!" says Duane. We follow the dogs to the front of the parade and climb onto the cart. We hide behind the sign as a man approaches. He attaches the handles of the cart first to Chessie's back and then to the back of a yellow Labrador. I glance behind us and see quite an array of dogs. Some are even in costumes. Following right behind us is a Cavalier King Charles Spaniel dressed like a lion. Behind him is a Husky dressed like a wizard! Music starts and I hear an announcer signal the beginning of the pet parade.

"Hold on tight and enjoy the ride!" Chessie calls back to us as she and the Lab begin leading the canines down the street. People line the sidewalks taking pictures and throwing treats just like Chessie said they would.

"Too bad they're dog treats," Duane says. "I guess nobody expected to see cats in the parade today. I wish they were throwing fish instead."

Just as he says this, I hear people in the crowd talking about us. "Look at those dogs! Boy, their owners did an amazing job dressing them up as cats!"

"They're talking about us, Duane," I tell him with a laugh. "They don't realize we really are cats!"

"I wish we could pretend to bark at them," he replies giggling. "It would really take them by surprise if we meowed!"

"Let's do it!" I say. "It'll be fun. What have we got to lose?"

Duane and I begin to meow as loudly as we can. This causes the dogs to bark. Pretty soon, there's a chorus of woofs and meows all the way down Thames Street. Some of the children in the crowd also begin making animal sounds! Before long, we come to the end of the road and Chessie turns to us.

"A group of us are going to go play in the dog area over at Patterson Park. Do you two want to come with us? Our owners are going to drive us there, but maybe we can sneak you in the car."

"Sounds good to me, but we can meet you there. Riley is a speedy cat. He can give me a ride," Duane says, looking at me with a grin.

I roll my eyes at him. "Climb on my back, Duane. I bet we'll even beat these guys in their car."

I can hear Chessie and the other dogs laugh as I take off down the road with Duane on my back. People laugh and shout at us as we run by. I think they've finally figured out that we're a couple of cats.

"Where am I going?" I shout up to Duane.

"See that green grass up ahead and all those trees?" he yells down to me. "That's where we're headed. The dog park is just a little further."

After spending the morning in the downtown area of Baltimore, being at the park feels so much different. There are lots of people around since it's a gorgeous fall day, but it feels so much more relaxed and peaceful. Runners are exercising on trails around the park while kids throw a frisbee back and forth in the grass. We cut across the field until we see a sign indicating we've arrived at the dog park.

"Way to go quickly, Riley," Duane says climbing off my back. "We beat the dogs. Here they come now."

Chessie and her buddies join us to play in the park. We run around, bat at one another, and play together until we run out of energy. When it's time for Chessie to leave, Duane and I lie down to rest in the shade of a tree.

"Looks like you had a lot of fun with those pups," a voice says from above us in the tree. I look up and feel like I'm looking into a mirror. Staring down at me is an orange tabby cat, but he's not quite as plump as I am.

"We sure did," I reply. "Have you been watching us this whole time?"

The cat nods, "I was relaxing up here in the tree when I saw you wander in with the dogs. I see a whole lot of dogs here but never any cats like me."

"We met them at the pet parade at the Fells Point Festival," Duane tells him. "We got to be part of it too."

"Oh, I think we're going to be good friends," the orange fluffball replies. "I love having adventures like that. My name is Killer."

"I'm Riley and this is Duane. Killer is an, um, interesting name," I say hesitantly.

Killer laughs, "No need to be frightened. I won't hurt you or anyone else for that matter. Can I show you around? I'll take you to my favorite place in the park and tell you how I got my name." He climbs down and jumps onto the ground next to us.

"Whoa! You can climb down trees! I thought I was the only cat in the world who could do that," I tell him.

"Cool!" he replies. "I thought I was the only one who could do it too. What about you, Duane? Do you have any special cat powers?"

Duane laughs. "Actually, I can jump really far. Between Riley's climbing and my jumping, that's how we escaped the house today to explore the city."

"Well, I guess we were meant to be friends," Killer says smiling. He begins to walk across the grass. "Follow me and I'll tell you all about the park. It has a pretty neat history. Back in the 1800s, soldiers defended Baltimore here during the War of 1812. It was used again during the Civil War, but that time as a hospital and camp for the Union soldiers."

"A lot of places down here have been used in wars," I tell him. "We explored Fort McHenry earlier and Duane told me all about the USS Torsk submarine."

"You really have been all over the place today," Killer replies.

"What's the big tower up ahead?" Duane asks.

"That's where we're going. It's the Patterson Park Pagoda."

"Pagoata? Is it full of goats?" I ask, puzzled.

"Pa-go-DA," Killer says, sounding it out for me. "No goats inside. In Asia these are used as temples. Here in Baltimore it's just a high tower to look out and see the city. Follow me to the top."

Killer and I climb up while Duane jumps from one tree branch to another. He leaps onto the top of the pagoda just as Killer and I arrive. It's not as high as the World Trade Center was earlier but it still gives us a really cool view of the city. We can see the line of buildings in downtown Baltimore with the water around them.

"I feel like I'm lying in the clouds when I'm up here," Killer says, closing his eyes and smiling. "It's just so peaceful."

"Can you tell us how you got your name, Killer?" Duane asks, lying back to relax.

"Sure! Killer wasn't my original name. I was first named Coppin because a nice lady found me at Coppin State University here in Baltimore. I was so little back then and she already had two cats, so I went to live with one of her friends. One day, while my new owner was at work, I was perched at the window. A huge flock of birds flew right in front of me and landed on the roof! I just had to get out there to see them. So, I scratched a little hole in the window screen and spent the day running around the roof with them. We had a lot of fun once they realized I didn't plan to eat them. They told me about all the places they had flown to and it made me crave those same adventures."

"That sounds a lot like my story," I say. "My very first adventure started because I met a seagull who made me wake up and explore with him."

"Seagulls can be very persuasive," Killer says.

"That's a great story, Killer, but it still doesn't tell us how you got your name," Duane says, encouraging him to continue.

"Right! Well, when my new owner got home, her neighbor told her she'd found me on the roof. She said 'that cat there is quite a killer.' I guess she hadn't realized I was just playing with the birds, not terrorizing them. Word got around about my day with the birds and soon after anyone who saw me started calling me Killer instead of Coppin. It's ironic because I've made so many friends now in Baltimore, both people and animals. I wouldn't harm a fly."

"That's a great story," I say. "Do you live really close to the park?"

"Not too far, but far enough that I had to hitch a ride on a delivery truck to get here today," Killer says grinning.

"Hey! I have a great idea," Duane says. "Would you like to spend the rest of the day with us? I think we're going to head back over to the Inner Harbor and check out the Maryland Science Center next. Want to come?"

"Absolutely, if you don't mind me tagging along," replies Killer. "How do you plan to get there?"

"The water taxi leaves from Fells Point and heads that way. If we go now we can probably catch the next boat," Duane replies.

"Sounds perfect," Killer says and the three of us make our way down the pagoda, climbing and jumping. As we walk together to catch our next ride, I can't help but think about how much my life has changed this past year. I went from being a common house cat who spent all his time inside, either playing with Jack or sleeping, to an adventure cat, exploring new cities and making lots of friends. I purr happily and smile at my new friends, excited about our next adventure.

Chapter 10
Science
Experiment

"Now this is a great way to ride!" I put my face up to the sun as the boat cruises along the water. We climbed aboard without being spotted and made our way to the roof. All three of us are lounging at the top enjoying the gorgeous weather.

"It sure is," Killer says, stretching out his legs. Duane has both of his front paws tucked underneath him, purring happily. We ride along silently until the water taxi docks.

"Let's jump off together," Duane says with a grin. "Climb onto my back since I'm the best jumper and we'll give the passengers a show."

Killer and I follow his directions and hold on tightly. Duane leaps from the roof of the boat and lands perfectly on the ground below. We look back to see everyone's jaws have dropped and a few kids are laughing. It was worth it to see the looks on their faces.

"This way to the Science Center," Duane says. He leads us down a walkway to a huge building.

It's rounded in the front with rectangular-shaped buildings pointing off from it. In front is a large metal display that resembles energy shooting off in every direction.

"Wow," I say as we get closer to the building. "This looks so cool! Do you have an idea of how to get inside?"

"I'm not sure. Let's get a little closer to the doors and check it out," Duane replies.

There aren't many people around the science center. As we approach the door, there's a big sign on it that says "Closed Today for Maintenance."

"Uh-oh. Now what? Do we just find somewhere else to go?" Killer asks.

"Come on, Killer. Are we going to let a closed sign stop our fun?" Duane asks. "We just need to be creative and find another way into the building." We all look around and then Killer points up in the air.

"Check that out, guys! A window is open on the top floor. Riley, you and I can climb easily. We could take Duane up to the window and then explore the science center from the top down!"

"Great idea! Hop on, Duane," I say. He climbs onto my back, holds on tightly, and up we go. When we're about halfway up, I glance down and see a little boy tugging on his mom's coat and pointing up at us. I laugh and continue my climb, wagging my tail a little. It's fun to be able to entertain people while enjoying time with new friends.

As if reading my mind, Duane says, "I've explored a lot on my own, Riley, but it's so much better doing it with you, and now Killer, too."

"I agree, Duane. I made so many friends when I was exploring Delmarva. Now I've made friends in Baltimore, too. Pretty soon I'll have buddies all over the world!" I exclaim.

Duane laughs, "I have no doubt you'll make friends anywhere you go. Alright, here's our way in," he says as we get to the window. I carefully climb inside and jump onto the ground.

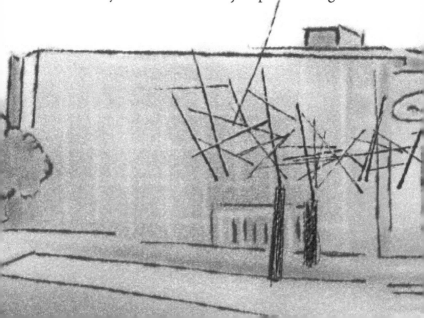

My eyes get wide as I look ahead. Staring back at me is the biggest crab I've ever seen.

"I don't like the looks of that," Killer says nervously.

"Let's approach it carefully and let it know we're nice," Duane suggests. We walk together slowly toward the giant crab. It is standing perfectly still as if waiting to pinch us at any moment with its ginormous claws. We get all the way up to the railing surrounding it and stare intensely at one another. All of a sudden, I hear a voice from behind me.

"You can stare at him all day, but he's never going to talk to you."

I turn around slowly and notice tanks along the walls that remind me of the aquarium.

"Over here!" the voice says from my right. Duane, Killer, and I walk toward the sound and I finally see who called out to us. He looks a lot like the giant crab, but he's much smaller and safely inside a tank.

"Hi! I'm Riley and these are my friends, Duane and Killer. You're a blue crab aren't you?" I ask him.

"I sure am. My name is Snuggles. I used to live in the Atlantic Ocean, but I've been here in this tank for a few months now. It's neat to see so many people, but I miss my friends and family back home," he says sadly.

"Snuggles? You wouldn't happen to know a crab named Cuddles, would you?" I ask excitedly.

"Are you kidding? Cuddles is my cousin! Do you know him?" he replies.

"Wow! What a small world! I met Cuddles when I traveled to Ocean City with my owner. He explored all of Delmarva with my seagull friend and me," I tell him.

"Cuddles?! Explored the town with a cat? No way," Snuggles says, looking at me like I'm crazy.

"I kid you not," I reply, holding up a paw to show I'm being honest. "He was scared at first, but we coaxed him out of his shell. Not literally," I add, laughing.

"That's amazing! I wish I could tell him I met you too," he says sadly.

"What if you could, Snuggles?" Duane says suddenly. We all look at him, puzzled. "Hear me out. What if we could get you out of this tank? You could explore the rest of the science center with us and then travel back to Ocean City to be with your family."

"That's a great idea, Duane," I tell him. "I know just how to do it, too. The top of your tank opens for easy cleaning and feeding. I'll get up there and reach my paw down as far as it can go. Snuggles, you can climb up the house there in your tank and then pinch my fur with your claw. I'll pull you up and out."

"Wow! Going back to my family really does

sound amazing. I'd love to see Cuddles again and hear all about his adventure," Snuggles agrees. "I'm willing to try it if you are. Let's go, Riley!"

I climb up to the top of the tank as Snuggles moves on top of the house. He loses his grip on my paw only once and then attaches firmly. I'm able to pull him up out of the water.

"Climb up my fur and I'll bring you down to the ground," I tell him. "Don't worry. You won't hurt me."

Snuggles follows my directions and before long I've broken him out of his tank and rejoined our friends on the ground.

"Well done!" Killer says. "Glad you are here with us, Snuggles."

"I really can't believe it," he says. "Never in my wildest dreams did I imagine three cats would help me return to the ocean. Now, what you do say we explore a little? I've been here long enough to know the fun things to do on each floor. Kids are always talking about the bed of nails downstairs. Let's head that way first!"

The other cats and I look at one another and I know we're all thinking the same thing. A bed of nails doesn't sound like fun but we silently agree to trust our new traveling companion. He stays on my back as we walk and points out some of the other exhibits.

"Over there is the Kids Room. Visitors are always talking about how much fun they have dressing up and playing with the toys in there. Oh, and there's the shed," he says, pointing to another room. "People go in there to invent all kinds of new things. What I hear them talk about is pretty neat. Let's head down these stairs though and I'll take you to 'Your Body.'"

"Is that where we're going to get poked by nails?" Killer asks. I was wondering the same thing.

Snuggles laughs, "Don't worry, Killer. It's harmless. Everyone is always talking about how exciting it is. You'll see," he adds when we still don't look convinced.

When we get to the second level, there is so much to see and do. We spend some time playing with wheels we can spin and toys we can move around. It's like a cat's playground! Even Snuggles is able to use his claws to pinch things. Finally, we make our way over to the bed of nails. A sign on the side explains how it works.

"That doesn't look so bad," Duane says, reading the sign. " We shouldn't feel any pain because the nails are spread out all over. It would be a lot different if we just had one giant nail poking us. The bed looks pretty big. Think we could try it out two at a time?"

Bravely, I step up. "I volunteer to go first. Who's with me?" I look around at my friends, hoping someone will be courageous enough to join me. Duane steps up.

"I'm in, cousin. Let's do it!"

We climb onto the flat bed and lie down. I can see the nails below me, but they aren't poking into us yet. I take a deep breath and muster up all of my courage.

"Ready?" Snuggles asks. He's standing next to the bed, ready to push a button. Duane and I look at each other and then nod at Snuggles. He uses his claw to push the button and then slowly the nails begin to rise. What a crazy feeling! I was expecting them to feel really sharp, but they don't hurt at all. Instead, it just feels like a bumpy blanket.

"Whoa! This is so cool!" Duane says. "It's actually comfortable."

"I know! I wasn't expecting that. I could stay here all day and just fall asleep," I reply.

"Don't get too comfortable, boys. It's our turn now," says Killer. Snuggles presses the button again and the nails slowly lower back down into the bed. Reluctantly, Duane and I climb off so that Killer and Snuggles can lie down. I take over the controls and when they give me the signal, I push the button with my claw. Slowly, the nails rise again. It's neat to see their reactions when they start to feel the points of the nails.

"Oh, wow! You guys weren't kidding. I've never felt anything like this before," Killer says.

"It feels a little prickly but in a good way," Snuggles agrees. I let them have a few more minutes lying on the bed and then I lower the nails.

"I feel super relaxed now," says Killer. "Let's go into that dark room over there. Maybe we can take a little nap."

We walk into a room called the Davis Planetarium. Killer was right. It is really dark inside. Good thing cats can see in the dark! After a few seconds, my eyes adjust and then I can see why it's called a planetarium. Stars and shapes are all around us. It feels like we've just stepped outside at night. I can see big circles that must be planets. One even has rings around it.

"That must be Saturn," Duane says, staring at the same planet I was looking at. "It has rings around it."

"Over here it says that Jupiter and Uranus have rings also," Killer says. "Look! Over there you can see the two other planets with rings. I wonder what all of these funny shapes are."

"It says here that they're constellations," Snuggles replies. "We're looking at Shapes in the Sky."

"Conversation? Do they talk?" I ask, puzzled.

"No, con-stell-a-tion," Snuggles sounds it out for me. "It says here that they're like pictures in the sky. If you were able to connect the stars with lines, then these would be the pictures you would see."

"This one over here looks like a bear," Duane says. "It has a giant bowl coming off its back."

"This sign says that's called the Big Dipper. It points up to the North Star, right over there," Killer says, pointing to a really bright star.

"That one looks like two people holding hands," I say. "The sign says it's called Gemini. Do you think we can find any cats?" We walk around the planetarium looking for animal constellations. Killer finds an eagle, Duane finds a snake, and I find a dragon.

"That one looks like me!" Snuggles exclaims suddenly, pointing to a group of stars in the shape of a crab.

"It really does, Snuggles. You'll have to find it in the night sky when you're back with Cuddles. You can always think of us when you see it," I tell him.

"Do you really think I can make it back to the ocean, to my family?" Snuggles asks.

"I absolutely do, Snuggles," Duane says. "Stick with us and we'll help you get on your way. Now, let's head downstairs and finish our time here so you can start your journey."

We follow Duane down to the first level and find ourselves surrounded by dinosaurs. A humongous T-Rex stares at us from above. We walk around, mesmerized, looking at dinosaur bones and digging for fossils. In one section, we play follow-the-leader and jump from one giant dinosaur footprint to another. Finally, we go across the hall into a huge movie theater. Seats are lined up in rows with a big screen in front that goes all the way from the floor to the ceiling. Killer finds a button to press and the screen comes to life. We watch and listen in amazement as a movie called *Backyard Wilderness* plays in front of us. It's incredible. The images appear as if they're in the room with us.

"This is wild," I whisper to Duane. I know nobody else is in the room with us, but I still feel like I need to talk quietly.

"I know! Look at that deer! It's running right toward us!" he replies, flinching a little. I know in my head that it can't really run off the screen, but it sure seems real.

"Watch out for the fox!" Killer yells as a group of foxes stroll by. I guess he thinks it's real also. We continue watching together as we jump with frogs, run with foxes, and fly with birds. It's pretty neat to see all of the animals that surround us outside. Before long, the movie ends and we make our way out of the science center.

"I loved exploring in there," I tell my friends. "I can't wait to tell Jack about the bed of nails!"

"I can't wait to tell Cuddles about the crab constellation," Snuggles says.

"Let's get you on your way, Snuggles," Duane says. "Your journey home is about to begin!"

"We're right here at the water," Killer says. "This leads into the Chesapeake Bay. You're going to have to follow the bay south until it meets the ocean, down in Virginia. You'll find a really long bridge there and that's how you'll know you've reached the ocean. From there, travel north along the coast until you get back to Ocean City."

"That doesn't sound easy," I say anxiously.

"No, it doesn't," Snuggles agrees, "but I can do it. I NEED to do it so that I can be back where I belong. You three went to the trouble of breaking me out of my tank. Now it's up to me to do the rest. I can't tell you how much I appreciate it."

"I'm so glad we could help," I say. "I believe in you, Snuggles. Your cousin, Cuddles, was such a brave crab. I'm sure it runs in the family."

"I can't wait to tell him I met you, Riley," he says. "Promise you'll come back and visit us someday in Ocean City."

"I will do my best," I tell him. "If my owner has another conference your way, I'll be there. I promise."

Killer, Duane, and I take turns saying goodbye to Snuggles and then I use my tail to slowly lower him down into the water. He waves a claw at us before departing for his long journey home.

"Good luck, Snuggles!" I shout as we watch him disappear into the water.

Chapter 11
Poetry and
Football

"Where to next?" Killer asks after we say goodbye to our crabby friend. The three of us are strolling along the water.

"I was thinking maybe we'd head over to M&T Bank Stadium and see if we could watch some of the Ravens game. Mom was talking with your dad about that before they left this morning, Riley," Duane says.

"I'm heading that way if you want to follow me," a voice says. We look around and then a black bird lands right on my head! I look up at him wide-eyed.

"Who are you?" I ask as he settles himself between my ears. I'm surprised he isn't afraid of cats.

"I'm Eddie. I've been watching you three for awhile now. I saw you walk all the way up the side of the science center and then saw you come out with a crab on your back. You don't seem like ordinary cats, so I figured you probably wouldn't eat me," he says.

"You're a smart bird," Duane tells him. "We are explorers, not hunters. I've been taking my cousin, Riley, all around Baltimore today and we met Killer over in Patterson Park. We'd love to go to the Ravens game with you."

"I knew you looked familiar," Eddie says, looking at Killer. "I've seen you around Hampden before, haven't I?"

"You probably have," Killer replies. "That's where I live. I spend a lot of time cruising all over the neighborhood, but sometimes my

adventures lead me other places which is how I ended up with these two today."

"Fun! I have some bird friends over that way. We like to go to the zoo and visit other animal friends there. You should come with us sometime."

"I would love to," Killer says.

"Is that where you live, Eddie?" I ask him.

"No. I live on the west side of Baltimore close to Edgar Allan Poe's grave. That sounds morbid, right?" he asks, looking at our scared faces.

"Why would you choose to live at a grave?" Duane asks, shivering in fear.

"You haven't put it together yet?" he asks us. When we shake our heads no, he explains. "I'm a raven bird. Edgar Allan Poe was a famous writer and poet. He lived in Baltimore for a few years and then moved down to Virginia. He traveled through our city a lot to visit his family and friends. He died and was buried here in Baltimore and there's a whole house and museum dedicated to him. One of his most famous poems was called 'The Raven.' A few years ago, a visitor saw me at the grave and named me Eddie, short for Edgar. She and her friends thought it was so neat that an actual raven was at the gravesite, so I made it my home. I entertain people whenever they come to visit."

"Wow, Eddie! What a neat story! I always wondered how the football team got its name. I guess it's named after the poem," I say.

"I like to think it's actually named after me," Eddie jokes. "Since you guys can climb and I can fly, we shouldn't have any trouble getting into the game. I'll introduce you to my buddy, Poe, when we get there. We need to hurry, though. The game is going to be ending soon."

Just as he says this, something catches my eye and I have a great idea. "How would you all like to ride in style?" I ask my friends.

"What do you mean, Riley? On another bus?" Duane asks.

"I was actually thinking we would do the driving this time," I reply with a grin. "Have either of you ever driven a scooter?"

"Oh! I've seen people ride those all around town," Killer says. "I've ridden on the back of one, but I've never driven one myself."

"I think we can figure it out. I drove something similar when I visited Delmarva. Let's check it out," I say, leading our group over to the electric scooters. I take some time inspecting them, but they look easy to drive.

"I'm willing to try driving, Riley," Killer says. "Duane, do you want to hop on with me?"

"Sure. I wouldn't mind just being a passenger for this," Duane says hesitantly.

"Perfect! I'll take this one. Eddie, you can either stay perched on my head or fly along with us," I say.

"I fly on my own all the time. I'll go for the ride this time," he replies with a smile.

I laugh. "Sounds good to me! Let's go!"

Killer and I pick out our scooters and I show him how to turn the throttle to fire them up. They roar to life.

"Follow me!" I yell over the noise. "Eddie will direct us to the stadium!"

Killer gives me a nod and I push off. The scooter easily glides forward. The roads are crowded so we see tons of people staring open-mouthed and pointing as we ride by. Eddie leads me toward the stadium, turning this way and that. I quickly glance behind me and see Killer riding along smoothly. He's a natural! We arrive at the stadium in no time at all, just as a roar goes up from the crowd. Hopefully something good just happened for the Ravens. I park the scooter and Killer slides in next to me.

"That was wild!" he says, climbing off and shaking himself out.

"What an incredible way to ride!" Duane agrees.

"Are you guys up for another climb?" Eddie asks. "If we head over this way, we can sneak into the stadium and be close to the end zone." The three of us follow our new bird friend. When he starts to fly up, Duane hops on my back and we begin climbing, with Killer right behind me. Everyone must be so into the game that they don't notice what we're doing.

"Success!" Eddie says as we reach the top. "Let's go down the ramp to get to the lower level. We'll be closer to the field that way."

We follow our leader and soon find ourselves back outside. Only this time we're in a sea of purple and black. Ravens fans pack the stadium to cheer on their team as they play their rival, the Pittsburgh Steelers. I glance up at the scoreboard and see that the game is tied 24 – 24 in the fourth quarter with only a minute left to play.

"There's my friend, Poe," Eddie says, pointing to a bird that looks like him, only a lot bigger. He's standing inside what looks like a nest. "He's the Ravens mascot. He's not a real bird so he can't understand us when we talk, but I've gotten to be friends with him anyway. The person inside the costume likes to talk to me."

"Is he standing in a bird's nest?" I ask Eddie as we head toward Poe.

"Yeah! Isn't that cool? He gets his own pretend nest at every home game."

We walk down to meet Poe, easily getting past the fans who are focused on the game being played. He does a double take when he sees our group. "Whoa, Eddie! You've never brought friends with you before. Cats, huh? Well, that's a first for a Ravens game. Want to watch the end of the game here in my nest?" he asks.

We all meow and Poe seems to understand that means yes. Killer, Duane, and I all perch on different sides of the nest while Eddie flies right up onto Poe's shoulder. He must do that a lot because Poe doesn't look surprised to see him there. All around us people finally start to notice that there are cats in the nest. I can hear them talking about us and see them pointing. Then all of a sudden, I hear a roar of excitement from the crowd followed by a loud whistle and then a chorus of boos.

"What happened?" I ask Duane.

"The Ravens looked as if they were going to score a touchdown, but the referees called the runner out of bounds just before the goal line," he explains.

"Wow, you know a lot about football," I reply.

"My mom and dad watch a ton of football. I usually sit on the back of the sofa and watch games with them. I've learned a lot. Like, now the players will run off the field and new ones will come on. See that guy down there?" he says, pointing to a player who lined himself up with the ball and then took a few steps back and over. "He's our kicker, Justin Tucker. He's scored the winning points for our team on many different occasions and it looks like he might do it again today."

All around us, the crowd is cheering for Tucker. The Ravens snap the ball and Tucker runs forward and kicks with all his might. We watch as the ball soars directly through the middle of the goal posts.

The announcer shouts, "The kick is good! Ravens win!"

The crowd goes wild and Poe starts banging on a giant drum. I look up at the huge screen and there's Poe, surrounded by 3 cats and a real raven.

"Look, guys!" I yell, pointing at the screen. "We're famous!"

Killer and Duane look up just as the announcer notices us. "I can't believe it. Poe has brought some new friends to today's game. I guess anything is possible. Let's hear it for Poe, our mascot, the three cats in his nest, and the raven on his shoulder. Thanks for bringing us luck today!"

We all sit up a little taller as the crowd cheers again loudly, only this time for us. Fans in the seats around us reach over to scratch our backs. Before long, the crowd starts to exit the stadium and, after meowing goodbye to Poe, we follow them out.

"I guess we don't have to climb out this time since everyone knows we're here now," Killer says as we walk through the stadium. People stop every now and then to say hello and pet us. It feels good to be celebrities.

"I think this is where my journey ends today, guys," Killer says as we leave the stadium. "I need to head home for dinner."

"Mind if I join you? Not for dinner, but for the trip to Hampden? I wouldn't mind seeing my friends over there. Maybe you'd like to visit the zoo with us tomorrow," Eddie says.

"Sounds great! Let's hop on the light rail to

get there. It's kind of like a small train," Killer explains.

"We'll walk over with you," Duane says. "Riley and I are going to finish our day at the Orioles game and that's right next to the light rail."

We all walk the short distance from one stadium to the other. I really don't like saying goodbye to so many new friends. It makes me sad to think I'll never see them again.

Eddie seems to read my mind. "Don't look so sad, Riley," he says. "Maybe we'll meet again someday."

"Yeah or maybe you'll meet one of my family members somewhere, just like we met Snuggles today," Killer chimes in.

"I hope so," I reply. "It was great to meet both of you. Thanks for taking us to the Ravens game, Eddie. And Killer, you keep having adventures too."

"I sure will. Now I have a raven buddy to tag along with me," he says smiling. Duane and I wag our tails as the cat and bird climb onto the back of the light rail. We stand and watch as it quickly rolls away, taking our new friends on their next adventure.

Chapter 12
America's
Pastime

"No more moping, Riley! Let's head over to the ballpark before it gets crowded. It's time for some good food and a different type of ball game. First stop, Boog Powell's Famous Barbecue," Duane announces. My tummy grumbles and I realize we have been doing so much that we've barely eaten today. Almost all I did was eat when I explored Delmarva!

"I have no idea what that is, but you haven't let me down yet, Duane. Lead the way!" I say.

Duane and I walk through a parking lot next to a giant brick building. "This is the B&O warehouse," Duane tells me. "It was used back in the 1960s to hold goods coming off the trains on the railroad."

"What's it used for now?" I ask, glancing up at the tall building.

"Mainly offices for the baseball team. Whenever my mom has a game on TV, I watch to see if someone will hit a ball far enough to hit the warehouse. It hasn't happened during a game yet, although I heard an announcer once say that Ken Griffey, Jr. hit it during the home run derby of the all-star game!"

We come to the end of the warehouse and find ourselves at the entrance to Oriole Park at Camden Yards. It feels like we're in another world. There are trees up and down the sidewalks and big black gates indicating the street name. The one in front of us says Eutaw Street. Big numbers are scattered around the front of the entrance.

"What are those?" I ask Duane, pointing at the numbers.

"Those are the numbers of famous Orioles who have retired from the sport," he says, leading me over to a giant number eight. "This is Cal Ripken, Jr.'s number. He played his entire career with the Orioles. His dad played, too. Let's go check out the other numbers."

Duane and I make our way around the area reading about the great Hall of Fame superstars from Orioles' history. As we start to walk down Eutaw Street and into the park, there are plaques that look like baseballs in various places on the ground. I walk over to one and read "Baltimore Orioles, Chris Davis, August 17, 2016, 395 yds."

"Hey, Duane! Check this out. I bet this is where a ball landed during a game. I've heard Chris Davis's name before."

"These are so cool!" Duane says, reading another. "Look over there! I see one on the side of the warehouse. That must be the one I was telling you about before."

We continue walking, checking out the baseballs as we go, when the most amazing smell hits my nose. I stop abruptly to breathe in deeply and Duane runs right into me.

"Oof! Why did you stop, Riley? See something cool?" Duane asks.

"I don't see anything but I sure do smell something," I reply. I follow my nose toward a big orange roof that says "Boog's BBQ: World Famous Pit Beef." It's on top of a stand featuring tons of food that both smells and looks delicious.

"This is what I was talking about earlier," Duane says as we approach the stand. "Remember this morning when you asked what a Boog was? Well, Boog Powell was a famous Oriole and now his pit beef is just as famous as he is. It already looks pretty busy. A lot of people stop here first before they head to their seats. Maybe we can slip behind unnoticed and get some scraps."

Duane and I wait until all of the servers are helping hungry customers. Then we sneak quietly behind the stand and find bits and pieces of pit beef that have been tossed aside. It's covered in a savory sauce that is just as delicious as it smells. We feast until our bellies are satisfied.

"You have a little sauce on your nose there, Riley," Duane says, laughing as he licks his paws.

I look, cross-eyed, down at my nose and can see what he's talking about. I swipe at it a few times with my paw and lick off the last bit of sauce.

"Mmmm, that's tasty," I tell him.

"You know what would go great with this? A snowball," Duane replies.

"A snowball? It isn't winter though. Where are we going to find snow?" I ask.

"It's not that kind of snowball, Riley. It's shaved ice with flavored syrup. It would be the perfect dessert after our pit beef dinner. There's a stand right over there," he says. "Let's go see if they'll give dessert to a couple of cats."

We walk over to the snowball stand and start to meow. The worker looks down at us in surprise.

"Well, this isn't something I see every day," he says as we meow cutely and begin to rub against his legs. We sure do know how to get strangers to like us. "Aren't you cute kitties? Just out here to watch a ball game, huh?" He reaches down and scratches Duane's head. I purr a little and then flop onto my back and look up at him. He runs his hand over me and says, "Don't worry, I have enough love to give both of you sweet guys." We have clearly won him over. Now we just need to get him to give us dessert.

As if reading my mind, he says, "How about some cold snowballs for my new cat friends?" We meow and watch him get to work. He takes two small cups and puts them under a machine that holds a giant block of ice. When he pulls a lever, the machine shaves ice off the block and into the cups. When the cups are full, he molds the top so it looks like a snowball. Then he takes it over to where he has a bunch of colored bottles.

"Hmm, which flavor would be best?" he says, looking around at the various colors. Finally he chooses one. "This is perfect," he announces as he squirts an orange liquid all over the snowballs. Then, he adds something white on top of each one. He puts them on the ground where Duane and I eye them hesitantly. "Don't be scaredy cats!" he says. "I chose Baltimore's favorite flavor for you—egg custard. Don't worry, it doesn't taste like eggs. It's a sweet flavor and it's one of the Orioles' colors, so that's an added bonus. I topped them off with a little scoop of marshmallow. Enjoy!"

He leaves us to our sweet treat and gets back to serving customers.

"Well, Duane, we haven't had a bad meal yet. Let's dig in," I say. We both take little licks of our snowballs. It is as cold as ice cream but doesn't feel the same. The ice is so soft and melts in my mouth. The worker was right— the egg custard flavor tastes sugary-sweet. I decide to try a little of the white stuff. It's really sticky! After a few licks, I can feel it all over my whiskers. I look at Duane and he is sporting a skinny, white, marshmallow mustache! We laugh at each other and continue to devour our snowballs. By the time we get to the bottom of our cups, I can hear the crowd getting louder. It must be close to game time.

"What do you say we go find some seats?" Duane asks, using his paws to get the last bits of marshmallow off his face.

"Sounds good to me," I reply as I take my final licks of dessert. We meow goodbye to the worker who is now frantically making snowballs for his customers. "What are those big yellow poles?" I ask as we start walking around the stadium again.

"Those are the foul poles. If a player hits a ball into the stands anywhere between those two poles, then it's a home run," Duane explains.

"I have a crazy idea, Duane," I say suddenly. "What if we climb to the top and watch the game from up there? We'd have a bird's-eye view of the stadium and I bet nobody would even notice us."

"That's a great idea, Riley. We'll be able to see everything from up there!" Duane replies. We walk over to the right field foul pole and he climbs onto my back.

"We're pros at this now, aren't we Duane?" I call to him as I start my ascent up the pole.

"We sure are. It's a good thing you can climb so easily, Riley. We've been able to do so many things today that we wouldn't have been able to do otherwise."

"It's a good thing I'm not too scared of heights either," I say as we make our way to the top. Duane carefully climbs off my back and we cling onto the top of the foul pole with our claws. The view from up here is incredible. I look out over the field and watch as the players warm up throwing and fielding. The stands are starting to become full of fans eager to cheer for their home team. Down on top of one of the dugouts, I see a big, black bird similar to Poe from the Ravens game, but not exactly the same.

"What do you think that bird is down on the dugout?" I ask Duane.

"That's the Oriole bird. He's the team mascot just like Poe is for the Ravens," Duane replies.

"He's not a real oriole," I hear a squeaky voice say just before landing on my head. I peer up and see a bird staring down at me. I seem to be attracting birds today. He's smaller than Eddie and has an orange chest with a black head and wings.

"Well, hello there. Who are you?" I ask, trying to be friendly.

"My name's Ike and you've discovered my favorite place to watch baseball games. I can see everything from up here. I perch on top of one of the foul poles during just about every game. This is the first time I've seen cats up here though," he says. "I thought cats were afraid of heights. Aren't you the ones who are always getting stuck in trees?"

"We aren't ordinary cats," Duane tells him. "My name is Duane and this is my cousin, Riley. He is skilled at climbing so he brought us up here to watch the game."

"It's nice to meet you, Ike," I say to the bird who is now sitting comfortably atop my head. "Let me guess. You're an oriole bird, aren't you?"

"That's right! Just like the mascot dancing down there on the dugout, only I can fly around and whistle and stuff," Ike says.

"Whistle?" I ask, confused.

"Oh, yes. That's one of the things we are known for. I love to perch high up in the treetops, whistling songs. Sometimes other birds join me and we sing together. It's easy to make friends when you're a bird," Ike says. Then he surprises us by whistling a little tune.

"That sounds so pretty," Duane says. "All we can do is purr and meow."

"Purring and meowing are pretty sounds too," Ike replies. "Oh, look! The game is getting ready to start."

We listen as someone sings the national anthem. It reminds me of this morning, standing at Fort McHenry while the anthem was played. Duane smiles at me and I know he's thinking the same thing. Then all of a sudden the entire stadium shouts 'O!' in the middle of the song.

"What in the world was that?" I ask Ike once the song is finished.

He laughs. "It's a Baltimore thing. In the middle of the national anthem, when the singer sings 'Oh,' the entire crowd of Orioles fans shouts it. It's a tradition that started back when the O's played at a different ballpark called Memorial Stadium. One woman shouted it during a game and the next night someone joined her. After that, it grew to include the whole crowd. Go to any sports venue in Baltimore and you'll hear that 'O.' It's just a way that the fans help cheer on their home team."

"We should totally meow during that part of the song the next time our owners are watching a game on TV, Riley," Duane says laughing. "They'd think it was hysterical."

We laugh and settle in to watch the game. The Red Sox take an early 3-0 lead over the O's, but that just makes our fans cheer louder. We get some hits throughout the game but don't have any luck scoring runs. Before long, it's the bottom of the 9th inning and an Orioles player, Trey Mancini, steps up to the plate. There are three Orioles on base hoping to score, but there are already two outs in the inning. Mancini watches the first ball go by. The umpire yells "strike!" He swings and misses the next pitch. I can tell that he is determined to bring his teammates home and win the game. The Red Sox pitcher winds up and throws a fastball to the inside corner. It's the perfect pitch for Mancini. He swings and connects! The ball goes soaring up into the sky into the outfield directly toward the right field foul pole.

"What do we do? It's coming right for us!" I shout to Duane and Ike.

"Get on my back this time, Riley. I'll jump out of the way!" Duane yells. I quickly do as he says, just in the nick of time. Duane leaps into the air while I cling to his back. Ike flies above us. The ball hits the foul pole exactly where we were sitting and then it falls to the ground. As we land back in our spot on the pole, the fans cheer louder than ever. The announcer yells "Grand slam homerun" as Mancini and his teammates round the bases. The Orioles beat the Red Sox 4-3!

"Whoa! It's a good thing you can jump, Duane. That ball would have knocked us right off this pole!" I say.

"No kidding! I know it's a home run when the ball hits the foul pole, but I wonder if it would

still count if it hit cats on the pole," Duane says. Then he yells, "Look!" He's pointing to the jumbotron where they're showing a replay of the home run. The camera follows the path of the ball and shows two cats jumping out of the way right at the last minute. The camera switches to real time and zooms in on us. I'm still on Duane's back and Ike is perched on my head. We meow for the camera and the crowd goes wild.

"Ending our day as celebrities at the Orioles game isn't so bad," I say to Duane. "We should probably head home, though, so we can get settled in before Aunt Kristin and Dad get there."

"Good thinking, Riley. Hey, Ike. Want to come with us?" Duane asks.

"Thanks for the invite, but I'm going to stick around here. Some friends of mine like to get together after a winning game so we can sing. The hometown crowd loves it. It was great to meet you though. This was so much fun tonight," Ike says.

"Thanks for hanging out up here with us, Ike. I hope I see you around again," Duane says.

"Have fun with your oriole bird friends," I say as Duane climbs onto my back for our trip down the pole.

"See you later, boys!" Ike says as he flies away.

Chapter 13
Just in Time

"What's the quickest way to get home?" I ask Duane as we walk out of the stadium. We were able to exit before most of the crowd left, giving us a good head start.

"The quickest or the safest?" Duane replies with a glint of humor in his eye.

"Uh, both?" I say carefully. What in the world could Duane have in mind?

"Come on, Riley. Where'd your sense of adventure go?" Duane jokes. "The fastest way is to hop on those scooters again."

"Well, that was easy before. Why won't it be safe this time?" I ask.

"Remember how we came across the water in a sailboat to get to Fort McHenry? We don't have time to wait for a boat now. This time we're going to need to go through the tunnel," Duane says.

"What exactly is a tunnel?" I ask nervously. Somehow I know I'm not going to like the answer.

"It's a road that goes under the water," Duane answers. "You know those tubes that our owners like to get for us and we run through them to play? It's just like those but it goes through water."

I don't like the sound of driving a scooter through the water, but if Duane thinks it's ok then I'll have to be brave. "Okay, Duane. If you're sure about this, then I'm in. Do you want to drive this time?"

Duane laughs. "You're the experienced driver, Riley. I'll hop on and direct you." We make our way to the scooters and I expertly start one up. Duane hops onto the back, points out where to go, and then holds on tightly with his claws. I guide our scooter down a sidewalk and see the highway up ahead of us. Mustering up all the courage I can, I steer us into the shoulder of the busy road.

You've done this before, Riley, I think to myself. You can do it again. Cars whiz by while I keep my eyes focused on the road in front of me. My instincts take over and I am able to block out the sounds of cars and trucks. Fortunately, Duane was right. I have become an expert scooter driver. The highway goes over the Patapsco River and then curves around. I continue to follow it past a park and can see Fort McHenry up ahead of me. The flag that I helped raise this morning is slowly being lowered for the night.

"There's the entrance to the tunnel," Duane shouts. I can see the road lowering down and water all around. I zoom toward the tunnel entrance and try to imagine that I'm playing in a cat toy tunnel in my living room at home. I think of Rick chasing us around the house this morning. I wonder what he would think of this. I can't wait to tell him all the stories from our day today. Thinking about that makes it easier to forget that I'm currently driving under a river. There are lights on the side of the tunnel that also help make it less scary. In no time at all, I can see the exit up ahead.

"Ever heard the phrase 'there's a light at the end of the tunnel?'" Duane asks. "There's the light!" I cruise out of the tunnel and breathe a sigh of relief. It's nice to have the water behind me now and the sky overhead. Duane continues to direct me until we are back in Aunt Kristin's neighborhood. I slow the scooter and we park it up the street from the house.

"How do you usually get back in, Duane?" I ask.

"You can climb back up to the window, Riley, but I usually jump," he replies before skillfully jumping from one tree branch to another. I climb up the tree and join him outside the window. Just then, I hear a car coming up the street and headlights flash toward us.

"Quick! It's Aunt Kristin and Dad! How do we get in?" I exclaim.

Duane meows loudly and instantly Rick is at the window. "Geez, I was starting to think you guys weren't coming back," he says as he pushes the screen open for us. Duane leaps inside and I follow behind him. Duane quickly adjusts the window as we hear the door opening downstairs. Rick flops onto the rug, Duane curls up on the chair, and I lie down on the sofa just as they come upstairs.

"Hey there, lazy boys. You're sleeping right where we left you this morning," Aunt Kristin says. I get up slowly and stretch as if I've been in that position a long time. Duane reaches his paws forward and yawns. We're surprisingly good actors.

Dad sits on the sofa next to me and runs his hand along my back. "Did you have a good time here watching birds with Duane?" he asks. I wish I could talk. I'd tell him we didn't just sit here watching birds. We met a couple and hung out with them!

"I still can't believe what happened at the O's game tonight," Aunt Kristin says, sitting next to Duane on the chair. She throws a toy down the hallway and Rick chases it.

"I know! The last thing I expected to see

was a couple of cats on the foul pole. They sure did look a lot like you two," Dad says to us. I meow innocently and roll onto my back. Rick looks first at Duane and then at me and I know he's wondering if it really was us. I see Duane wink at him.

"I'm going to head up to bed," Aunt Kristin says with a yawn.

"I'll follow you up. I'm exhausted," Dad says. "Coming, Riley? Or are you hanging with your cousin tonight since we're going home tomorrow?" In response, I jump over to Duane's chair and cozy up next to him. Dad laughs. "I guess that's my answer. Goodnight, buddy," he says before following Aunt Kristin upstairs.

Rick obediently follows his owner but glances back at us. We're going to have to fill him in on our escapades tomorrow.

Duane stretches out next to me and sighs. "This was an incredible day, Riley. I was excited when I heard you were coming to visit, but I had no idea what an adventure this day would be. I just thought we'd terrorize Rick all day."

"I thought the same thing, Duane. I knew I wanted to get out and explore, but I had no idea how I was going to do it. I'm so lucky to have a cousin who's just as daring as I am."

"We're just two extraordinary cats," Duane replies. "And extraordinarily tired. Goodnight, Riley."

"Goodnight, Duane," I say as he drifts off to sleep. I watch him for a few minutes and think about what an amazing day we had together. I met so many new friends and explored another incredible city. I wish I could tell my friend Bagel all about my experiences in Baltimore. Maybe someday, I think to myself. For now, I'm just happy that I kept my promise to him. As I snuggle up next to Duane and drift into dreamland, one thought stays in my mind.

Where will my next adventure be?

About the Author

Allison Wiest was an elementary school teacher for 12 years but has had a passion for writing since she was young. In 2018, she left her teaching position to finally write the story that had been developing in her head for over five years. *Roaming Riley: A Delmarva Adventure*, published in 2020, earned an Honorable Mention in the Purple Dragonfly book awards and was a Finalist in the National Indie Excellence Awards. Allison grew up in the suburbs of Baltimore so it was fitting that Riley would explore Baltimore City next. She hopes to continue the Roaming Riley series so Riley can explore the world. Allison currently lives in Selbyville, Delaware with her husband, two daughters, three cats, and a dog. For all the latest news, check out www.allisonwiest.com or follow her on Instagram at allisonwiest_author.

CPSIA information can be obtained
at www.ICGtesting.com
Printed in the USA
LVHW010250250222
711932LV00007B/1298

9 781628 063370